For my mom and dad,

thanks for giving me
the joy of a puppy
and the love of a dog.

Cover and illustrations by Zoe Saunders.

Paperback ISBN: 979-8-9876859-0-7
Hardback ISBN: 979-8-9876859-1-4

Published by LMM Publications.

Words by
Lynn Matchett

Illustrations by
Zoe Saunders

Daisy stretches and yawns as a patch of sunshine peeks through the window and warms her fur.

Snap, snap, snap,

go her ears as she quickly shakes her head.

Daisy scoots on her belly and uses her nose to lift a resting hand.

She begins each day with Mom petting her soft brown ears.

Daisy runs to the door.

Click, Clack.
Click, Clack.

Her ears perk up like a flower in the rain
and her tail thumps the floor like a tiny drum.

Daisy squirms and twists as Mom clips her leash.

Daisy floats through the air as Mom lifts her up so she can kiss her soft brown ears.

Daisy bounces along
on her little legs.

Flap, flap, flap,
go her ears like happy butterfly wings.

She stops.

She stares.

One ear shoots up.

Flick, flick, flick,

goes the bushy tail
of a nearby squirrel.

Daisy freezes.

Her back legs wobble.

She's ready to bark.

But she turns to mush when Mom whispers words of love and pets her soft brown ears.

Daisy slurps from her bowl.
Her paws tap a happy dance of relief.

Splash, gulp. Splash, gulp.

The wispy ends of her ears take a dip.

Mom giggles.

She brings Daisy close and dries her soft brown ears.

Daisy is curious.

She smells something new and her nose twitches.
She stands on her back legs to see over the edge.

"Uh-oh!"

Crash, crash.

Ting, ting.

Daisy is still as her eyes follow Mom.
Her ears droop low and hide her face.

Mom tells Daisy she still loves her
and pets her soft brown ears.

On the way to town, Daisy sticks her head out the window.

Whoosh, whoosh, whoosh,

the wind blows.

Her eyes water and her whiskers bend.
Her ears are flipping from front to back, inside and out.

Daisy relaxes on the seat and Mom reaches over to pet her soft brown ears.

Daisy shivers as the sun goes down.
She wiggles her way onto Mom's lap.

Circle, circle, circle,
plop.

She stretches and yawns.
Her ears lie still and she closes her eyes.

She breathes in and out with whispering snores.

Daisy snuggles close and drifts into a dream
with Mom petting her soft brown ears.

Follow Daisy to Find Pages to Color!

Daisy

About The Author

Lynn Matchett lives in Indiana in the United States with her husband and two sons. She is passionate about reading, writing, playing the piano and animals. She is the director of a non-profit organization that provides dental care to children in schools. Working with children each day has inspired her to pursue her lifelong dream of becoming an author.

Follow Lynn on Instagram @lynnmatchettwriter

Ingram Content Group UK Ltd.
Milton Keynes UK
UKHW051254070423
419793UK00004B/27